for Bibi, Tessi and Merlin — G.T.
for Bethany Boo — S.V.

Text copyright © 2004 by Ginette Thomas. Illustrations copyright © 2004 by Susan Varley.
The rights of Ginette Thomas and Susan Varley to be identified as the author and illustrator of this work
have been asserted by them in accordance with the Copyright, Designs and Patents Act, 1988.

First published in Great Britain in 2004 by Andersen Press Ltd., 20 Vauxhall Bridge Road, London SW1V 2SA.
Published in Australia by Random House Australia Pty., 20 Alfred Street, Milsons Point, Sydney, NSW 2061.
All rights reserved. Colour separated in Switzerland by Photolitho AG, Zürich.
Printed and bound in Italy by Grafiche AZ, Verona.

10   9   8   7   6   5   4   3   2   1

British Library Cataloguing in Publication Data available.

ISBN 1 84270 326 9

This book has been printed on acid-free paper

The VOLE Who Would Be KING

story by Ginette Thomas
pictures by Susan Varley

Andersen Press
London

The tiny vole stood on the Royal Rock in the middle of the forest, stuck his chin in the air and squeaked as loudly as he could,

"Today I will be king."

It wasn't long before Rabbit came hopping along.

She stopped and looked up at the vole.

"Hello, Vole. Don't you know that's the Royal Rock? What are you doing?"

"Oh, I'm just standing here, filing my nails, waiting for the King of the Forest. When he comes I'm going to tell him that *I'm* the new King of the Forest."

Rabbit thought that Vole was being very silly indeed and she hopped off quickly, back towards her hole.

A little while later, Hedgehog came shuffling along.
He stopped and looked up at the vole.

"Hello, Vole. You'll get into terrible trouble standing on
the Royal Rock. What are you doing?"

"Oh, I'm just standing here, filing my nails, waiting for the King
of the Forest. When he comes I'm going to tell him that
I'm the new King of the Forest."

Hedgehog thought that Vole was being very silly indeed and he
shuffled off and hid under a huge pile of leaves.

A few minutes later, Fox came trotting along.
He stopped and looked up at the vole, licking his lips.

"Hello, Vole. Don't you know whose rock you're standing on?
I think you should come down here."

"Oh no, I won't," replied Vole. "I'll carry on standing here,
filing my nails, waiting for the King of the Forest.
When he comes, I'll tell him that *I'm* the new King of the Forest."

Fox stopped licking his lips. He thought that Vole was being very silly
indeed and he trotted off quickly to a patch of thick undergrowth,
where he curled up and hid.

Vole had not been standing on the Royal Rock for very much longer when he noticed something happening . . .

The leaves on the trees began to shake.
The ground began to shake.
The Royal Rock began to shake
and Vole himself began to shake!

Along came the King of the Forest.
He was the biggest, blackest,
fiercest-looking bear you ever did see.
He was as tall as the tallest tree.
He had claws sharper than the sharpest
knife and his teeth were as big as you!
His voice boomed like thunder.

"Who's standing on my rock?"

He bent down to take a closer look.
He couldn't see very well because he'd lost his glasses.
"Vole, what are you doing on my rock?"

Vole squeaked in his squeakiest voice, "Oh, I'm just standing here,
talking the biggest load of nonsense you ever did hear!"
And with that he jumped off the Royal Rock and dived
straight between King Bear's legs.

But before he could escape, a huge paw scooped him high in the air.
Vole was sure that King Bear would gobble him up.
Vole closed his eyes and waited. He waited and waited.
Nothing happened. Slowly he opened one eye, then the other.
In front of him was the biggest smile he had ever seen.
King Bear was actually smiling at him.

"So you want to be king, do you?" boomed King Bear.
Vole was too frightened to answer.
"You'd better sit up here then."
And, ever so gently, King Bear lifted Vole up and placed him inside the little gold crown that perched, a little lopsided, on top of his head. Vole clung on to the crown for dear life and peered over the edge.

King Bear began to walk through the forest and with every step the gigantic bear took, poor little Vole was thrown up and down inside the crown. But he clung on tightly and continued to peer over the edge.

Suddenly Vole cried,

"Stop!"

King Bear stopped with one foot in the air.
"Don't tread on the undergrowth. Fox is hiding in there."

Because he couldn't see very well without his glasses, King Bear
stooped down to take a closer look. Sure enough, he saw Fox's
bushy tail poking out from under the leaves and ferns.
Ever so carefully, he stepped over Fox's hiding place.

"Thank you, Vole," he said, and they carried on through the forest.

Suddenly Vole cried out again,

"Stop!"

King Bear stopped with one foot in the air.
"Don't step on those leaves. Look! Hedgehog's under there."

King Bear stooped down to take a closer look.
Sure enough, he saw Hedgehog's shiny black nose poking out
from beneath the pile of leaves.
Ever so carefully, he stepped over Hedgehog's hiding place.

"Thank you, Vole," he said, and they carried on through the forest.

Suddenly Vole shouted out again.

"Stop! Look out!"

King Bear stopped with one foot in the air.
"Don't tread on Rabbit!"

King Bear stooped down to take a closer look. Sure enough there was
Rabbit, so petrified that she was frozen to the spot.
King Bear, ever so gently, lifted Rabbit in his enormous paw and
put her down safely, out of harm's way.

"Thank you, Vole," he said, and they continued to walk through
the forest, with Vole still holding on to King Bear's crown very
tightly indeed.

Eventually they arrived back at the Royal Rock.
Ever so carefully, King Bear lifted Vole from his head and placed him down where he could see him properly.

"Vole, you have been very helpful to me today.
I would like you to be my Official Royal Looker-Outer.
What do you say?"

Vole was very proud indeed. He stuck his chin in the air and squeaked as loudly as he could,

"Yes please, King Bear."

Then suddenly, from behind King Bear came the loudest clapping and cheering you ever did hear . . .

King Bear turned around and there behind him were
all the animals of the forest.
There were animals everywhere,
and right at the front stood Rabbit, Hedgehog and Fox
who were clapping and cheering the loudest of all.

"Vole, our hero!" they all cried together.

And even though Vole wasn't the King of the Forest,
he thought that being a *real hero*
was every bit as good!